SNAFFLES
THE CAT BURGLAR

ReadZone Books Limited

www.ReadZoneBooks.com

© in this edition 2015 ReadZone Books Limited

This print edition published in cooperation with Fiction Express, who first published this title in weekly instalments as an interactive e-book.

FICTION EXPRESS

Fiction Express
First Floor Office, 2 College Street,
Ludlow, Shropshire SY8 1AN
www.fictionexpress.co.uk

Find out more about Fiction Express on pages 90–91.

Design: Laura Durman & Keith Williams
Cover Image: Hunt Emerson

© in the text 2015 Cavan Scott
The moral right of the author has been asserted.

ISBN 978-1-78322-543-9

Printed in Malta by Melita Press.

SNAFFLES
THE CAT BURGLAR

CAVAN SCOTT

What do other readers think?

Here are some comments left on the Fiction Express blog about this book:

"I have just read this book and I'm really enjoying it, it's just so funny! I really like this book and can't wait to read more."
Lucy C, student, Cardiff

"I like reading Snaffles the Cat Burglar. *Bonehead is funny."*
Scarlett Scott, student, London

Snaffles the Cat Burglar *is an amazing book and I love it. This book is funny, original and very interesting."*
Faith Elizabeth, student, Cardiff

"I am enjoying Snaffles. All of the chapters are funny!"
Grace, student, Coventry

"We loved reading Snaffles the Cat Burglar. *Thank you for writing an epic story. We can't wait for him to return!"*
4Believe at Low Moor C of E Primary School, Bradford

Contents

For Chloe and Connie

Chapter 1

The Purr-fect Crime

The glow from a full moon streamed through the skylights in the high roof of the London Museum of Shiny Stuff. In the room below, the Sensational Salmon of Sumatra – one of the world's most famous treasures – sparkled in its reinforced glass case.

All was still and all was calm… until one of the skylights creaked open. A furry head poked through the gap and peered down at the priceless plunder. The masked face was followed by an athletic body, squeezed into a tight jet-black outfit… a catsuit, you might say.

This, dear reader, was Snaffles – the greatest Cat Burglar in the history of nicking things.

If burglary had been an Olympic sport, Snaffles would have won every gold medal going. (Actually, he would have just *stolen* every gold medal going. He couldn't help himself. If something valuable wasn't nailed down, Snaffles would steal it – and if it *was* nailed down, he'd still pinch it… and the nails as well.)

Snaffles raised a slender paw to his ear. There was a soft click as he activated his hidden earpiece.

"Target in sight old boy," he whispered, his voice smoother than silk that has been vigorously pressed by the World Ironing Champion.

"I'm going in!"

Without waiting for a response, Snaffles leapt through the skylight and plummeted down towards the Sensational Salmon of Sumatra.

He wasn't falling, of course. You don't get to be the world's greatest cat burglar without being more stylish than that. Snaffles descended on an ultra-thin, hyper-strong cable that was connected to the back of his outfit. Everything about this crime had been planned to the smallest detail. The timing. The distance. The speed of descent.

Snaffles was a very clever thief.

Unfortunately, his assistant was not. This assistant couldn't even spell clever.

Not even if he had a dictionary in front of him with the word 'clever' highlighted in yellow and underlined three times.

Sadly for Snaffles, this brainless buffoon was in charge of the winch that controlled the ultra-thin, hyper-strong cable.

WHAM!

Snaffles slammed head first into the floor, cracking two tiles and at least three of his teeth. Worse of all, he also managed to bend his perfectly waxed whiskers out of shape. This just wouldn't do!

"Bonehead!" he yelled into his radio after he'd stopped seeing stars, "You were supposed to stop me BEFORE I hit the floor!"

"Was I, boss?" barked a confused dog-like voice over Snaffle's earpiece. It was dog-like mainly because Snaffle's addled assistant was in fact a bulldog.

"I thought you said I should stop you *after* you hit the floor!" Bonehead said.

"Why would I say THAT?" Snaffles boggled, pushing his bruised body back up to its aching feet.

"I did think it was a bit odd," Bonehead admitted.

"Winch me up," the cat burglar snapped and was instantly yanked back into the air, coming to a halt beside his glittering prize.

A smile stretched across Snaffles' face. The Sensational Salmon of Sumatra was even more spectacular than he'd hoped. All week crowds had gathered at the

Museum of Shiny Stuff to 'ooh' and 'ahh' over its beauty. Carved out of solid gold, the flamboyant fish had a glittering array of emeralds, rubies and sapphires for scales. It was simply stunning, and worth a fortune.

Snaffles pulled a shiny laser-cutter from his belt and cut a perfect hole in the Salmon's glass case. Carefully slipping his hand inside, he reached for the precious treasure. He had to be careful. The stand upon which the fantastic fish rested was packed with tiny pressure sensors. If disturbed, alarms would blare in every police station across the city.

Ha! Snaffles thought. *Mere child's play!*

In one fluid movement, he whipped the Salmon from the stand and replaced it immediately with a large can of cat food – his calling card. The can wobbled for a second and then balanced, perfectly matching the treasure's weight.

"Success!" Snaffles cried into the radio, hugging the Salmon to him. "Bonehead, take me up!"

Within seconds, Snaffles was whizzing back up towards the skylight, faster and faster.

Too fast, in fact.

"Bonehead, slow down!" Snaffles ordered, but Bonehead didn't answer.

WHOOSH! Snaffles shot through the skylight and into the night air.

This wasn't right.

Snaffles looked up. There, hovering above him was a police helicopter. Hanging from the chopper was a large hook that was, in turn, attached to an excited-looking bulldog. Bonehead was clutching the winch that was connected to Snaffles' ultra-thin, hyper-strong wire.

The bulldog waved at Snaffles as if this was the most normal thing in the world.

"Bonehead," Snaffles screamed into his radio. "What's going on?"

"Great plan, boss," chuckled Bonehead. "We've never made a getaway by helichopper before!"

"What are you talking about? This is *not* part of the plan!" Snaffles yelped back.

"Eh?" said the bulldog, scratching the back of his neck, which was a sure sign that he was confused. Bonehead scratched his neck a lot.

"Of *course*, it isn't," Snaffles spluttered. "It's the old bill!"

"The who?"

"The fuzz!"

"The what?"

"THE POLICE, YOU PEA- BRAINED POOCH!" Snaffles screamed.

"Oh," said Bonehead. "Oh dear."

"Exactly," Snaffles said, desperately trying to think of a way to escape.

It was then that Snaffles realized they were dropping… towards one particular window… in one particular house… in one particular street.

One particularly famous street.

Snaffles flew through the window of 10 Downing Street and landed in a heap on a very expensive rug.

Chapter 2

The PM's Problem

Snaffles looked up, still clutching the Salmon, and found himself staring straight into the face of the British Prime Minister.

The Prime Minister was about to extend a hand to Snaffles when he suddenly burst into tears!

Snaffles didn't have time to be confused. The door to the office burst open and a red-faced man with a ludicrously large moustache stomped in, dragging Bonehead behind him.

"Bonehead, you were supposed to be my guard dog," the cat said, hands on hips and whiskers twitching in anger.

"S-Sorry boss," Bonehead whimpered, giving Snaffles his saddest doggy-eyes. "Would it help if I bit this bloke? Oh, please let me bite him. Please, please."

Bonehead liked biting people. It was his third favourite pastime after catching fleas and chasing parked cars.

Snaffles looked the moustachioed newcomer up and down. "Somehow, old boy, I don't think it would do any good."

"I've waited a long time for this," the beetroot-faced man said, grinning triumphantly. "The World's Greatest Cat Burglar caught red-pawed… by *me*!"

"And who might *you* be?" Snaffles enquired.

"*I* am Admiral Theodore Grandchops," said the red-faced man.

"Sorry, my dear fellow, I've never heard of you," Snaffles sniffed dismissively.

"That's because he's the head of the Ministry of *Secret* Shenanigans," wailed the Prime Minister, before blowing his nose loudly on a pile of important-looking international treaties.

"What's wrong with him?" asked Bonehead, pointing at the sobbing statesman.

"Two days ago, someone very dear to the PM was abducted," the admiral revealed. "Snatched from this very room, in fact."

"How dreadful," said Snaffles. "A member of the family, I assume?" He glanced at the picture of the Prime Minister hugging two slightly embarrassed-looking children.

"Yessss," bawled the Prime Minister. "Poor little Gorgy. One minute he was running around his little wheel like normal and the next he was gone!"

Snaffle's ears twitched. "I beg your pardon?"

Spotting the cat's confusion, Admiral Grandchops explained, "Gorgonzola is the Prime Minister's beloved pet mouse… And he's been stolen."

"Not by me, I assure you," insisted Snaffles, who two days ago had been busy stealing the crown from the Statue of Liberty. Seriously, have a look. No-one has realized it's even gone yet!

"We know it wasn't you, you feline felon," said Grandchops. "But we need a master thief to solve the mystery of how the little squeaker was snatched from one of Britain's most secure buildings. In short, Snaffles, we need *you*!"

"So, the Smashing Salmon of Summertime was just a trap!" realized Bonehead in a rare moment of not getting *everything* wrong.

"Clever!" said Snaffles, impressed.

"Thanks!" said Bonehead, touched.

"Not you," said Snaffles, annoyed.

"Oh," said Bonehead, disappointed.

"So, what do you say?" the admiral asked. "Are you on board?"

Snaffles eyed the admiral suspiciously. "You want me – a cat – to track down a mouse. You do realize that cats and mice don't, how shall I put it, always see eye-to-eye?"

Grandchops nodded, his titanic 'tash bobbing up and down. "We believe you're the right puss for the job."

"I see," said Snaffles, twirling his whiskers. "And if you don't mind my asking… why should *I* help *you*?"

"That's easy," the admiral explained. "Either you find Gorgonzola or we'll throw you in prison for a hundred years."

"That's a looong time, boss," whispered Bonehead. "I'd be…" he started counting on his fingers… then gave up, "really old by the time I got out!"

Snaffles rolled his eyes before giving in to his fate. "Oh very well. I suppose we'd better start looking for clues."

"But where?" asked Bonehead, adding another neck-scratch to the day's ever-increasing tally.

"Well there's *that* for a start," Snaffles said, spotting something interesting on the other side of the room…

Chapter 3

Rat Rampage!

"What? Admiral Grandchops blustered, his moustache quivering in anticipation. "What the devil have you seen man, er, I mean moggie?"

"Only a giant robot rat peering through the Prime Minister's window!" sniffed the furry felon.

Everyone in the room whirled around (except for Bonehead who somehow always found himself looking the wrong way). Snaffles was right. There at the window was a gigantic metallic rat face that Snaffles could only imagine was connected to an equally gigantic metallic body.

Red eyes glared at them from above a long steel nose that bristled with sharp-ended steel whiskers. Beneath the whiskers snarled a steel mouth, complete with a row of jagged steel teeth… there really was a lot of steel!

"What does it want?" whimpered the Prime Minister, his knees knocking together so fast that Bonehead had started dancing a little rhumba to the beat.

Without warning, the robot rodent turned to stare at the Prime Minister. Laser beams suddenly shot from both its crimson eyes, smashing through the window.

The petrified politician was only saved by Snaffles leaping forward to knock him out of the way.

"I believe that answers your question, sir!" Snaffles gasped, as they tumbled to the floor.

"Get the Prime Minister out of here!" yelled Grandchops, much to the surprise of Bonehead who still hadn't noticed anything was wrong.

"Why, what's he done?" the dumb dog said at the precise moment a laser beam hit him squarely in the rear.

"YOW! My tail!" he shrieked, leaping so high that he cracked his head on the ceiling. Luckily, the ceiling came off far worse, as Bonehead's bonce is the thickest thing on earth (yes, thicker even than your mum's custard)!

"What are we going to do?" Bonehead asked, crashing back down on to his blackened behind. "Shall I sneak out and bite it, boss, shall I, shall I?"

"I doubt that would do any good, old chum," said Snaffles, performing a perfect backflip to avoid another sweep from the rat's laser gaze. The beams slammed into the back wall, leaving a trail of smouldering wallpaper in their wake. "You'd probably break those gnashers of yours. Besides I don't believe it's after the Prime Minister at all!"

"It's demolishing my office!" the PM squeaked from his hiding place beneath the desk. Charred papers floated down to the floor around him.

"Yes, but only because it's trying to get to *me*!" announced the cat burglar.

"This is no time to be big-headed," Grandchops scolded as he tried to poke the robot through the window using the tip of his umbrella.

"I'm not!" Snaffles insisted, as the Admiral's brolly burst into flames, singeing the fingers of the Ministry of Secret Shenanigans. "But I *am* right. Watch this!"

The ginger cat somersaulted into the air, bouncing off Bonehead's head to propel himself towards the priceless chandelier that hung from the ceiling.

At this time the enormous robot was trying to rake its way through the wall itself with cruel curved claws. As Snaffles jumped it turned its head, its lasers following the cat burglar's path through the air. The chandelier shattered instantly. Shards rained down as the acrobatic cat leapt from his crystal perch at the very last moment.

"That's at least one of my nine lives gone," the cat panted, wrinkling his nose. The smell of scorched fixtures and fittings was almost as unbearable as the Prime Minister's terrible tie. "Admiral, where's your helicopter?"

"Still hovering above Number 10," Grandchops replied. "Why?"

Claws popped from Snaffles' fingers and toes as he raced to the window. "Mind if I take it for a spin?"

Before the Admiral could respond, Snaffles jumped on to the ruined window ledge and started climbing up the black brickwork of the building.

"Hey, wait for me," yelled Bonehead. Grabbing hold of his boss's ginger tail, the hound swung out of the window, accidently kicking the giant rat right between the laser eyes.

"That's what you get for trying to roast my rump," the dog grinned. But as Snaffles scaled the wall, the rat swatted at them with its terrible claws, knocking fresh holes in the brickwork with every swipe.

Chapter 4

Helicopter Hi-jinx

High above our two heroes, the police chopper hung in the air, rotors whirring. A rope ladder tumbled down and Snaffles made a grab for the bottom rung.

"What are you waiting for, boys?" Snaffles shouted up. "Take us away!"

The pilot didn't need telling twice. With a whup, whup, whup, whup, the helicopter soared into the air, away from Downing Street and its armour-plated attacker.

"Ha!" Bonehead yelled down at the robot as it gnashed its metallic teeth. "If you're so clever, why don't you come after us?"

As if to answer the simple-minded sidekick, the rat's flail-like tail went rigid, and began to spin around and around and around. Grinning horribly, the massive mechanical menace was propelled into the sky.

"Whoops!" gulped Bonehead as Snaffles continued clambering up the ladder. "Me and my big mouth!"

"Don't worry, old bean," Snaffles said as they climbed into the helicopter. "We needed to get that thing away from Number 10 anyway."

"We did?" Bonehead asked, scratching the back of his neck. Then suddenly a rare expression crossed his face – as if a lightbulb had turned on inside his brain. "I mean, of *course* we did, boss," he smiled, then frowned as the lightbulb went out again. "But what are we going to do now?"

"Trap a rat, what else?" Snaffles announced, rudely pushing the helicopter pilot out of his seat. "Mind if I take over, old chap?"

Without waiting for permission, Snaffles grabbed the control stick and yanked it to the left. The chopper lurched into a tight turn, banking high over the Thames.

"Is that metallic monster still on our tail?" Snaffles yelled over his shoulder.

Bonehead poked his head through the side door, his tongue lolling in the wind like a dog hanging out of a moving car's window. Sure enough the rat was right behind them, laser eyes trying to blast their whirling blades with every turn. "Yup, boss. It's catching up too!"

Snaffles pushed the stick away from him, dropping the nose of the helicopter.

"Woah!" Bonehead cried, nearly tumbling out of the chopper as it dived down. "Watch it, boss!"

"Sorry, old fruit," Snaffles shouted back. "I've just had a 'wheely' good idea."

Bonehead turned to look out of the cockpit window and his eyes went wide. They were zooming straight towards the London Eye, the giant Ferris wheel that stood on the South Bank of the River Thames.

"We're going to c-c-c-crash!" Bonehead shrieked, jumping into the arms of the nearest policeman.

"Not today," Snaffles hissed through gritted teeth, pulling the stick back sharply. The nose of the helicopter pulled up with it, just in time to soar over the top of the huge wheel.

Behind them, the robot rat gulped as it realized its mistake. It was flying too fast to stop itself ploughing into the London Eye with an almighty…

CRASH!

Snaffles brought the helicopter about to see the steel squeaker snared in the Ferris wheel's spokes.

"Ha!" he laughed. "That's one in the *Eye* for our rotten rodent."

The cat burglar brought the helicopter

level with the trapped robot, blinding the beast with the chopper's searchlights. With a flick of a perfectly manicured claw, Snaffles switched on the helicopter's loudspeakers.

"This is Snaffles," he announced, his silky voice booming over the South Bank. "Master thief, pilot extraordinaire and bestselling author of 'How To Be Humble When You're Pretty Brilliant Already'. Who sent you to destroy me?"

"Yeah, and to shoot my bottom, too!" added Bonehead.

The rat's only answer was a maniacal laugh that could be heard all across London.

"That's for me to know," a thin voice cackled from the robot. "And for you to NEVER to find out, *Snuffles*!"

"Snaffles!" the cat burglar corrected.

"Whatever," said the voice, as strange blue lights started to dance along the robot's limbs like electricity. "Engage self-destruct mechanism!"

"NO!" Snaffles called, but it was too late.

With an almighty FZZZZZZZZZZZZZZ the robot disappeared into a cloud of dust, leaving a Ferris wheel full of shaken tourists furiously snapping pictures of Snaffles' bemused face.

"So what now?" Bonehead asked, scratching the back of his neck… again.

Snaffles pulled back on the stick, steering the helicopter across the Thames. "That is a very good question, Bonehead."

"It is?" Bonehead replied. He wasn't used to asking very good questions… or even good questions for that matter. "You're not expecting me to come up with a good answer, I hope?"

A smile spread across Snaffle's furry face. "I think I know who is behind this, old chum."

"You do?" replied Bonehead, who was always amazed when anyone knew anything.

"Yes," Snaffles said. "The greatest criminal mastermind that ever lived, other than me, of course."

Chapter 5

Professor Wicked-Whiskers

Snaffles brought the police helicopter down outside the imposing walls of one of the most famous buildings in Britain – The Tower of London.

"I don't get it," said Bonehead, leaping out of the chopper as the blades slowed to a stop. "I thought we were visiting your greatest anemones, boss. I can't see any flowers here."

"*NEM-E-SIS*," corrected Snaffles. "It means enemy, numbskull. This is where he lives."

"In the Tower of London?" Bonehead asked.

A luxurious black limousine screeched to a halt beside them. A door opened and Admiral Grandchops clambered out.

"Where better to lock up a prisoner," the chubby head of the Ministry of Secret Shenanigans snapped, smoothing his straining waistcoat, "than one of the oldest prisons in the land?" Grandchops gazed proudly at the impenetrable grey and yellow walls. "Nabbed the felon myself, when he was trying to steal Buckingham Palace."

"Steal *what*?" the bulldog boggled. "No one could pinch an entire palace. That's just silly."

"Not when you're Professor Wicked-Whiskers, the so-called greatest villain of his age," sniffed Snaffles, striding towards the entrance. "Shall we go in?"

* * *

Admiral Grandchops led Snaffles and Bonehead into the Tower. He nodded sharply at the Beefeater guards standing either side of the entrance in their pristine red and blue uniforms. The portly spymaster marched up to an enormous tapestry of King Henry VIII eating a large chicken leg, and cleared his throat.

"Harry," he called into the air. "This is Admiral Theodore Grandchops requesting access to the Top Secret, Highly-Classified, Don't-Tell-Anyone-About-It Vault."

Henry VIII's eyes flashed red as a computerized voice boomed around the walls. "WHAT IS THE PASSWORD?" it asked.

The admiral paused, stroking his moustache. "Oh, it's a tricky one… I can never remember it." He clicked his fingers. "Ah yes, of course, that's it." He placed his hands behind his back, leant towards the portrait of Henry and whispered in his ear. "The password is: password!"

"CORRECT!"

"Worst password ever!" Snaffles sniggered. "Only an idiot would forget that."

"Yeah, too right, boss," Bonehead agreed, before leaning in closer. "What was it again?"

The tapestry of Henry VIII rolled up to reveal an ornate carved wooden door.

This slid aside to reveal a studded leather door, which in turn slid aside to reveal a heavy iron door, which opened to reveal a dimly lit corridor.

"Can't be too careful," Grandchops said, stepping over the threshold.

"ENJOY YOUR VISIT TO THE TOP SECRET, HIGHLY-CLASSIFIED, DON'T-TELL-ANYONE-ABOUT-IT VAULT," Harry the computer said as Snaffles and Bonehead followed. "DON'T FORGET TO STOP AT OUR GIFT SHOP ON THE WAY OUT!"

"Oooh, gifts!" squealed Bonehead, clapping his paws together.

"This way," barked Grandchops, leading them down the corridor and unlocking the big double doors at the end of it.

"Professor Wicked-Whiskers is held in a state-of-the-art cell. Designed it myself. It's completely inescap–"

As they peered into the chamber at the end of the corridor, Professor Wicked-Whiskers' state-of-the-art and completely inescapable cell was completely and utterly… empty!

"He's escaped!" the admiral exclaimed, bounding forward. The cell itself was a large cube of transparent glass, furnished like a rather posh hotel. A plush bed sat beside a comfortable leather armchair and tall wooden bookshelves. "Harry, sound the alarm! The prisoner–"

"Is right behind you, Theodore," said a calm, well-mannered voice behind them.

Snaffles turned to see a short, grey-haired hamster stroll into the chamber. He was wearing a crimson smoking jacket, a rather unconvincing toupee and had a pair of half-moon glasses perched on the end of his twitching nose. "There's no need to get that moustache of yours in a twist," he said. "I just stepped out for a breath of fresh air."

Snaffles grinned as the aged hamster opened a secret door in his completely inescapable cell and slipped back inside. "There, is that better?" he asked.

Admiral Grandchop's mouth bobbed opened and shut like a gasping goldfish.

"Snaffles, you fiend," the hamster said, settling back into his armchair. "I thought you'd forgotten all about your arch-enemy Wicked-Whiskers!"

"As if we could, eh Bonehead?" Snaffles said to his sidekick – although to be honest the puzzled pooch was still struggling to remember the admiral's password.

"So, tell me, what's brought you crawling in here to me?"

The old hamster glared through narrowed eyes as Snaffles explained about the Prime Minister's missing mouse and the robotic rat that had attacked 10 Downing Street.

When he'd finished, Professor Wicked-Whiskers pushed his glasses up his furry nose. "It's an interesting tale," he said. "But I don't see what it has to do with me. I hope you don't think that *I* abducted Gorgonzola."

Snaffles laughed. "As if! You're the villain who tried to melt the moon using a high-powered laser beam–"

"Strapped to the back of a giant mutant pigeon, yes," Wicked-Whiskers remembered, smirking. "It would have worked if the flying pest hadn't been distracted by that pesky birdseed factory!"

"Exactly," Snaffles scoffed. "I mean, mouse-napping the Prime Minister's pet? It's beneath you. And anyway, how could you do it…" he flashed a mischievous glance at the admiral, "when you're so safely locked up here?"

Wicked-Whiskers chuckled. "Well, this mouse-napping business obviously has you stumped. Otherwise, you wouldn't be trying to charm me into helping you." He glared at Snaffles, making him feel like a naughty little schoolboy… or school-kitten… or whatever. "I'll tell you this for nothing," he went on. "I smell a rat – or at least some sort of rodent."

"You see, admiral," Snaffles said, turning back to Grandchops. "I knew the professor would be able to help."

But Grandchops wasn't there. Instead, he was making a dash for the double doors.

"Grandchops?" Snaffles asked, confused. "Where are you going, man?"

"As far away as I can get from you furry freaks," he grinned, pressing a button on the corridor wall. "Thanks for walking straight into my trap! Now you'll never get out, *or* find the stupid PM's precious pet! Bwah-ha-ha!"

Chapter 6

Betrayed!

The doors of the chamber slammed together. Snaffles leapt forward, trying to prise them apart with his claws, but they wouldn't budge.

"The traitor's locked us in," Snaffles snarled. "But why?"

Before anyone could answer, the floor began to tremble beneath Snaffles' feet, followed by the walls and then the ceiling. Dust started to cascade down from the rafters as the entire room shuddered.

"I knew I shouldn't have skipped breakfast," said Bonehead, patting his stomach.

"That's not your tummy rumbling, you mindless mutt," snapped Snaffles. "It's more like an earthquake!"

By now, the shaking had got so bad they could hardly stand, let alone walk.

"There must be some way out of here," said Snaffles, checking the brickwork around the doors for a hidden switch. "If not, we'll just have to batter them down."

"You'll be lucky," said the professor, hurrying out of his completely inescapable cell. "Those doors are bomb-proof. Nothing can break through them."

Snaffles wasn't having that. "I'm sure we can find a way out if we work together."

"*Me* work with *you*?" huffed the hamster.

"Yes, just for the time being, old bean," explained Snaffles. "This situation needs us to use our heads." His eyes went wide as an idea struck him. "Or, more precisely, *his* head." He turned towards his faithful sidekick.

"My what?" the dog asked, scratching the back of his neck.

Snaffles turned to the professor. "Bonehead's skull is the thickest thing on the planet," he said. "Maybe even in the entire universe."

Wicked-Whiskers frowned. "Are you suggesting we use your canine co-worker as a battering ram? What a fantastic idea!"

Bonehead laughed. "Oh no, no, no," he said. "The boss would never do that, would you boss?"

Five seconds later, Snaffles and the professor were swinging Bonehead headfirst at the double doors.

"I still, OUCH, don't think, OOF, this is, EEK, a good idea," Bonehead yelled as his head smashed into the doors.

"I mean, OW, it really, YIKES, hurts," he pointed out as they backed up and tried again.

"And the professor, OOH, said nothing's hard enough, ARGH, to break through these, EEE, doors," he concluded as they tried for a third time.

"We made it," Snaffles cheered as they broke through the doors and raced back down the quaking corridor.

"Thank goodness," Bonehead sighed in relief, but his face swiftly fell again when he saw the iron door at the other end of the corridor.

"Er… Harry," Snaffles yelled as he was thrown against the wall. "Open these doors! Now!"

"WHAT IS THE PASSWORD?" the computer replied.

"Ooh, what was it again?" Bonehead said, scratching his chin (which at least made a change from his neck).

"*Password*!" shouted Wicked-Whiskers impatiently as the iron, leather and wooden doors slid aside.

Snaffles followed his arch-nemesis, as he staggered over to a window. "I don't believe it!" he gasped.

Outside the Tower of London, Beefeaters were running for their lives, followed by a large flock of flapping ravens. Beneath the building, thick black smoke was billowing out from its very foundations.

"This isn't an earthquake," Snaffles gasped. "Someone's installed rockets underneath the Tower of London."

"What was that, boss?" yelled Bonehead, pointing to his ears. "I couldn't hear you over the sound of the rockets that someone's installed underneath the Tower of London."

All at once, Admiral Grandchops' voice rumbled from a hidden loudspeaker.

"Prepare for take-off!" the traitor bellowed, triumphantly. "10, 9, 8, 7…"

"We need to get out of here," Snaffles shouted, trying to make for the exit. Instead, he was thrown from his feet as the rockets prepared to fire.

The admiral's countdown continued. "6, 5, 3…."

"What happened to four?" Wicked-Whiskers cried.

"AH YES! 4, 3, 2, 1! BLAST OFF!"

All around the capital, tourists gaped in shock as the entire Tower of London took off like a massive stone rocket!

"So *that's* how you steal an entire building," Bonehead gasped as they sped higher and higher into the sky!

"Where on Earth… or even *off* Earth… is the old duffer taking us now?" Snaffles cried, holding on to the windowsill as if all eight of his remaining lives depended on it!

Chapter 7

What goes up…

"Don't like it, don't like it, DON'T LI-EE-I-EE-I-EE-IKE IT!" yelled Bonehead as the Tower of London rocketed higher and higher into the sky. The three animals were flattened to the floor as the shuddering one-thousand-year-old building threatened to rip apart around them. The Tower's medieval makers had obviously never expected their creation to be blasted into the clouds.

"Hang on, old boy," Snaffles shouted back. "I think we're changing direction."

Sure enough, the Tower levelled off, zooming over the west of England before heading across the Bristol Channel. Before you could say 'what goes up, must plummet down', the flying fortress was soaring across the Atlantic Ocean towards America.

"Boss!" Bonehead blurted out as they tumbled across the floor to land against the far wall. "OOPH! I didn't bring my passport! How will we get through customs?"

"I think they'll be more interested in the sudden arrival of a London landmark than your lack of paperwork," snapped Professor Wicked-Whiskers. "Snaffles, what are you waiting for? *Do* something!"

"I'm thinking," the feline felon barked back – which was quite an achievement for a cat – but he didn't have to think for long. Without warning the rockets cut out and the Tower started dropping towards the water!

"I hate water!" Bonehead wailed as the three abductees rolled down the wall towards the ceiling. "ARPH! I don't even like taking a bath!"

"Obviously," added the professor, wrinkling his nose as he clutched his unconvincing toupee to his head. "Just hold your breath!" he cried, his cheek pouches growing as he gulped a giant breath of air.

"Hold it with what?" Bonehead yelped, wide-eyed.

SPLASH!

The Tower of London plunged into the ocean, sending up a gigantic plume of spray in its wake. Water poured through the windows and under the doors. If Bonehead hated flying in a world-famous fortress he soon hated sinking in one even more. As the water flooded in, Wicked-Whiskers scrambled up on to Snaffles' head, the cat burglar leaping on to Bonehead's shoulders. And as for Bonehead himself? The poor pooch was already underwater!

Snaffles took a deep breath, filling his lungs with as much air as possible before his head disappeared beneath the inky black sea. He let go of his canine companion and scrabbled for his belt, barely able to feel his furry fingers let alone the secret compartment he needed.

There you are, Snaffles thought as he found his trusty torch and flicked the switch.

A beam of light cut through the gloom, picking out Bonehead trying to doggy paddle. To his right, Wicked-Whiskers seemed to be fiddling with his toupee.

Is this really the time to check your wig is on straight? Snaffles thought with annoyance.

Then the professor's toupee did something Snaffles had never seen a toupee do before. With a yank of a hidden ripcord, the wig started spinning on Wicked-Whiskers' head. Snaffles opened his mouth in amazement, shutting it again quickly as a bubble of air escaped.

The wig wasn't just a rubbish-looking hairpiece – it was an emergency propeller *disguised* as a rubbish-looking hairpiece! Professor Wicked-Whiskers thundered towards an open window like a tiny hairy torpedo. As he barrelled past, Snaffles grabbed the hamster's leg, snaking his own tail around Bonehead. The three of them shot out of the Tower of London just as the capsized castle crashed into the sea-bed with a deep, muffled…

BOOM!

As they rose back to the surface, Snaffles tugged at his nemesis's trouser leg and pointed frantically at a huge shadow that loomed towards them.

It's a shark! Snaffles thought in dismay. *Or maybe a whale!*

In fact, it was neither of those things. The speeding object was a gargantuan submarine, shaped bizarrely like a huge wedge of Swiss cheese. Portholes pitted its steel sides, searchlights all but blinding them in the gloom. Wicked-Whiskers tried to manoeuvre out of the way, but it was too late. The thin edge of the wedge split open and swallowed the three of them whole.

Chapter 8

Like Rats in a Trap

Snaffles spluttered as he broke the water's surface. They had been washed down a tunnel and into large tank. As he looked around, bright yellow lights glared down from a low ceiling. Beside him, Wicked-Whiskers was also gasping, while Bonehead's big bottom stuck into the air, stubby legs pedalling like mad. Sighing, Snaffled pulled on his sidekick's tail and Bonehead flipped over in the water.

"Thanks boss," Bonehead wheezed, before spitting out what looked like half the contents of the Atlantic Ocean, including two prawns and a halibut!

"Don't thank me… yet," Snaffles said, looking up warily. Hulking figures glared at them from the metal walkway around the tank – an army of robot rats. Metal teeth gnashed, red eyes flashed and thick tails swished behind their bulky bodies.

"YOU WILL COME WITH US!" they shrieked as one, their voices as pleasant as a choir of dentists' drills.

"Shall I bite 'em, boss?" asked Bonehead, "Do you think that would help? Do you? Do you?"

"Of course it wouldn't, you idiot!" snapped the professor, much to Snaffles' annoyance. No one called his best friend an idiot – except for Snaffles, of course. Glaring at the rude rodent, the cat burglar leant across and yanked at the ripcord dangling from Wicked-Whiskers' toupee. The propellor immediately kicked into life, shooting the helpless hamster into the air.

"THE PRISONER IS TRYING TO ESCAPE!" yelled the robotic rodents, their tails whipping into action. "STOP HIM!"

"This is our chance, old boy," hissed Snaffles, grabbing Bonehead's collar and dragging him towards a metal ladder. Snaffles hauled his soggy sidekick out of the tank and made for a circular doorway. "Come on!"

Bonehead hesitated. "What about the professor?"

"What about him?" Snaffles asked,

glancing over his shoulder. The hamster was held tight in a net of rats' tails, terror written all over his furry face. Snaffles' heart sank. No matter how much he despised his arch-enemy, no one deserved such a fate – not even Wicked-Whiskers!

Snaffles plucked three tiny silver spheres from a pocket on his belt and threw them towards the rats. They exploded in mid-air, bathing the tank room in brilliant white light. As the rats' optical sensors overloaded, Bonehead scooped up his boss and hurled him towards Wicked-Whiskers. Snaffles snatched the professor, pulling him free of the tangle of tails and flipped over, cat and hamster landing gracefully on the other side of the gantry.

"Let's get out of here," Snaffles shouted as they raced around to rejoin Bonehead. But their escape bid was short-lived. Bonehead shrieked as a giant rat cage dropped down around them with a loud, resounding CLANG!

* * *

Snaffles, Bonehead and the professor were carried through the submarine, each wrapped tightly in a rat's tail. The robots marched through a pair of wide doors into the sub's control room. There, inside an enormous mouse-wheel, the British Prime Minister was being forced to run faster than a fox chasing a rabbit on roller skates. He looked exhausted.

As Bonehead gaped at the panting politician, Snaffles sniffed. "Whatever's that awful smell?" he asked, screwing up his nose.

"It's not me," Bonehead quickly pointed out. "At least, I don't think so!"

Snaffles looked down. "Crimp my whiskers, you're right, old chap!" The three adventurers were being suspended over what looked worryingly like a vat of bubbling molten mozzarella cheese.

"A-ha!" said a familiar voice. "I see you have spotted my vat of bubbling molten mozzarella cheese!"

Snaffles looked up to see Admiral Grandchops waddle out from behind the Prime Minister's wheel.

"I should have known you were behind all this, you rotter," the cat burglar snarled. "I bet you mouse-napped Gorgonzola as well!"

"Of course I didn't," the tubby traitor guffawed. "I mean, how could I mouse-nap myself?"

Grandchops pulled open his shirt to reveal a shiny metal midriff.

"You're… you're a robot, too!" Snaffles gasped, but there was another surprise still to come. With a series of whirrs and clicks, a tiny door opened in the admiral's steel chest, revealing a small mouse pulling levers and pressing buttons!

"Gorgonzola, I presume," Snaffles enquired.

"That's funny," sniggered Bonehead. "We're actually looking for a mouse called Gorgonzola! What a coincidence!"

"*I'm* Gorgonzola, you canine cretin!" the mouse crowed. "The fake kidnapping was just the beginning of my despicable plan!"

"*Whose* despicable plan?" demanded Wicked-Whiskers as he was gently lowered to stand beside Gorgonzola.

"*Ours… our* idea, of course," the mouse simpered.

"I knew I shouldn't have trusted you, Wicked-Whiskers!" Snaffles hissed. "Double-crossing is your middle name!"

"Actually it's Susan," the professor smirked, readjusting his toupee. "Well, who did you think had designed all these wonderful toys?"

"But *why?*" Snaffles asked. "Why go to such lengths?"

"That's for us to know and you to find out," the professor chuckled, before changing his monstrous mind.

"Actually, thinking about it, you never will…."

Snaffles didn't like the sound of that. "Why not?"

"Because I'm about to drown you in my Cheesy Pit of DOOM!" the mouse squeaked in triumph.

The professor cleared his throat loudly, and Gorgonzola rolled his eyes. "I mean, *our* cheesy pit of Doom!" he added through gritted teeth. "Throw them in! Throw them in NOW!"

Chapter 9

The Cheesy Pit of Doom!

The rats' tails twitched as the robot rodents prepared to drop our heroes into the Cheesy Pit of Doom.

"Bonehead, old bean," Snaffles called. "You know you've been wanting to bite something for days?"

"Yes, boss?" the dog replied.

"Now's your chance!"

"Yes, boss!" Bonehead grinned before sinking his gnashers into the tip of his captor's tail.

The effect was instantaneous. Electricity arced up and down the flailing tail, the robotic rodent going into a frenzy as its circuits sizzled. Bonehead juddered as hundreds of volts passed through his body – his glowing doggy skeleton suddenly visible through his fur – but refused to let go, jaws clenched tight. Of course, in any other animal, this would have fried its brain, but in Bonehead's case… well.…

Now, a lot of things happened in the next few seconds, so bear with me as we run through the course of events step-by-step:

1. With a final computerized wail, the short-circuiting rat cracked its tail like a whip, the end breaking off in Bonehead's mouth.

2. The still-shuddering sidekick was hurled across the pit, slamming straight into Admiral Grandchops – or the fake robotic Admiral Grandchops, at least.

3. The impact threw Gorgonzola out from behind his controls and into his Cheesy Pit of Doom.

4. The bulldog rolled head over heels until he finally crashed into the Prime Minister's giant wheel, which toppled over, handily trapping Wicked-Whiskers.

(Keeping up so far? Good, cos there's still four more to go…)

6. Gorgonzola disappeared beneath the bubbling surface of the Cheesy Pit of Doom with a big wet PLOP!

7. "WE MUST RESCUE THE MASTER!" the robot rats chorused as the mouse sank without a trace.

8. The robots, one with Snaffles still attached, began to dive into the cheese like a team of sinister synchronized swimmers, their joints immediately fusing in the boiling, gloopy mess.

9. The stupid writer realized that he'd missed out number 5. Never mind, it wasn't important anyway.

What was important was the fact that it looked as if Snaffles might end his days in a steaming vat of molten mozzarella and mechanical monsters. However, as his ratty captor leapt into the vat, the fearless feline whipped out the very same laser-cutter he'd used to steal the Sensational Salmon of Sumatra (remember?).

Before you could say: 'it's lucky you still had that in your utility belt, old sport!', Snaffles had cut himself free. Using one of the sinking rats as a stepping-stone he bounded to safety, landing beside the overturned wheel to find a slightly singed Bonehead pulling the Prime Minister from the wreckage.

"What now, boss?" Bonehead asked as the exhausted Prime Minister tried to work out whether to have a nervous breakdown or not.

"We skedaddle," Snaffles announced, rushing out of the control room in search of an escape pod. "Follow me, chaps!"

Chapter 10

Missile Mayhem

There was only one problem. Gorgonzola and Professor Wicked-Whiskers had been so convinced their plan was foolproof, that the fools hadn't bothered to install escape pods in their Swiss-cheese sub. Instead, our heroes found themselves in a room full of large, deadly missiles.

"I don't like the look of those," Snaffles said, rushing to a bank of computers.

"I don't like the smell of 'em," Bonehead said, sniffing one of the pointed metal tubes.

The Prime Minister just sat down in the corner and had a little weep.

Snaffles checked a screen: "Twist my tail, they're packed full of quick-hardening Double-Gloucester… but that's not the worst of it. Wicked-Whiskers has programmed them to target every major city in the world. Washington DC, Moscow, Paris – even Swindon! They'll all be buried beneath the stinky orange cheese when the missiles hit!"

"So what do we do, boss?" Bonehead asked, giving his neck the most vigorous scratch yet.

"Surrender!" came a voice from behind. They whirled around to find Professor Wicked-Whiskers pointing a gigantic blunderbuss in their general direction. "Paws up where I can see them!"

Glowering, Snaffles raised his hands, although the tip of his tail was still secretly tap-tap-tapping at the computer controls behind his back.

"OK, you win," Snaffles murmured, much to the surprise of Bonehead who had never heard his boss give up before. "Especially when you're holding such a big gun."

"Oh, this isn't a gun," sneered the hamster. "It's the mobile molten mascarpone mega-cannon™!"

"Another of your ingenious inventions?" Snaffles asked.

"My best yet," beamed the professor. "One pull of the mobile molten mascarpone mega-cannon™ trigger, and you and your pathetic pooch will be completely 'cheesed off'!"

He paused to chuckle at his own joke (which would later win the highly sought-after Worst Supervillain Pun of the Year contest).

"You wouldn't dare," piped up Bonehead, drawing a surprised look from Snaffles.

"What are you doing, you muddled mutt?" he hissed.

"Trust me," the dog replied, blinking at his boss as he'd never quite mastered winking with one eye. "I bet that thing doesn't work anyway."

"Does too!" the professor snapped back.

"Does not!" Bonehead replied, which was the nearest he ever got to a witty comeback.

"Does too!" Wicked-Whiskers responded, now completely dragged down to Bonehead's level (which was a very low place indeed!).

"Show us then!" Bonehead goaded the professor, puffing out his chest defiantly. "Shoot us where we stand!"

"With pleasure!" the professor sneered, pulling the trigger without another word. A stream of sticky white cheese shot out of the end of the mobile molten mascarpone mega-cannon™, but before Snaffles was completely splattered, Bonehead leapt forward and opened his mouth. The cheese flowed straight down his gullet as he guzzled it up by the gallon.

"Good work, old boy," Snaffles cried out, turning back to the computer and reaching for a large red button labelled 'ABORT!'

"Now, I just have to press this, and Wicked-Whiskers' cheesy missiles will be disarmed!"

He slapped his paw down on the button. Sirens wailed and lights flashed.

"Bwa-ha-ha-haaaaa!" Wicked-Whiskers laughed as all around mechanical grabbers started loading the missiles into their tubes. "Fooled you!"

"What's happening?" Snaffles asked, innocently, his tail still at work behind him.

The submarine trembled as one by one the missiles were launched, screaming out of the ocean into the skies above.

"I've beaten you, that's what?" crowed the professor. "Because I'm such a clever evil genius, I disguised the launch button as an abort button, just in case a thief-turned-secret-agent broke into the submarine to foil my plans! The world is doomed!"

"Oh really?" smirked Snaffles as a computer screen blazed into life, displaying the path of the missiles. "I don't think so. You see, I realized straight away that you had disguised the launch button as an abort button. I'd expect nothing less from my arch-nemesis. So, I reprogrammed the missiles' course!"

He glanced up to check his handiwork. One by one, the missiles flipped over in the sky and rocketed back towards the submarine.

"Noooooooooo," Wicked-Whiskers screamed, dropping the mobile molten mascarpone mega-cannon™ in despair.

"The world is saved!" Snaffles concluded, polishing his claws against his chest. "Unlike you!"

"Or us," burped Bonehead, who had ballooned to twice his size after scoffing so much cheese.

"Your dim-witted dog is right for once," Wicked-Whiskers jeered. "You'll be blown up with me!"

"I think not, old chap," Snaffles said, producing the professor's toupee from behind his back. "They don't call me the world's greatest cat burglar for nothing!"

"My propeller-wig!" Wicked-Whiskers screeched as the missiles closed in on the sub. "You no-good, flea-bitten, common thief!"

Snaffles slapped the toupee on his head and pulled the hidden ripcord.

"Oh, I think you'll find there's nothing common about me!"

BOOM!

The torpedoes slammed into the submarine, instantly encasing Wicked-Whiskers' underwater base in a ball of quick-hardening dairy produce – but not before a certain ginger cat propelled himself back to the surface, dragging his super-sized sidekick and a completely addled Prime Minister to safety.

* * *

"Britain owes you its thanks, Snaffles," said Admiral Grandchops later that day in the headquarters of the Ministry of Secret Shenanigans. "As does the entire world."

This, just in case you were wondering, was the *real* Admiral Theodore Grandchops, not a cheap metallic knock-off built by Professor Wicked-Whiskers. The poor spymaster had been tied up in the Ministry's toilets the entire time, hoping that someone would find him soon (not the least because he was desperate for a… well, you know what I mean).

"It was nothing," said Snaffles, brushing away the gratitude in a rare moment of modesty.

"Easy for you to say," groaned Bonehead, clutching his stomach. "I never want to see another crumb of cheese again."

Snaffles chuckled before asking: "And what of the Prime Minister?"

"He's taking a well-deserved holiday," Grandchops said, pulling a photo from a file on his desk, "with his new pet!"

Snaffles took the picture. It showed the Prime Minister, cuddling a fish bowl containing a startled-looking goldfish.

"Much better than a mouse!" Snaffles nodded in approval.

"Especially on toast!"

"And what about us?" belched Bonehead.

Grandchops fished out an important-looking scroll. "By order of Her Majesty's Government, both of you are hereby pardoned for all past crimes."

"And future ones?" Snaffles asked hopefully.

"Don't push it!" Grandchops said with a smile. "Oh, and that's not your only reward. I would like to present you with

the Sensational Salmon of Sumatra....
I think you've earned it!"

The spymaster turned to the shelf that had, until a few seconds ago, housed the priceless treasure. "Good heavens, it's been stolen! Again!"

"Of course it has," said Snaffles from the open office window where he and Bonehead were already making their escape. "By Snaffles the world's greatest cat burglar no less! Toodle-pip!"

And with that, Snaffles and Bonehead leapt from the window, off on another adventure. Well, at least Snaffles leapt. Bonehead sort of toppled, arms flapping like a demented bird, but you can't have everything....

THE END

BUT SNAFFLES THE CAT
BURGLAR WILL RETURN!

FICTION EXPRESS

THE READERS TAKE CONTROL!

Have you ever wanted to change the course of a plot, change a character's destiny, tell an author what to write next?

Well, now you can!

'Snaffles the Cat Burglar' was originally written for the award-winning interactive e-book website Fiction Express.

Fiction Express e-books are published in gripping weekly episodes. At the end of each episode, readers are given voting options to decide where the plot goes next. They vote online and the winning vote is then conveyed to the author who writes the next episode, in real time, according to the readers' most popular choice.

www.fictionexpress.co.uk

WINNER
Education Resources
Award for Innovation

FICTION EXPRESS

TALK TO THE AUTHORS

The Fiction Express website features a blog where readers can interact with the authors while they are writing. An exciting and unique opportunity!

FANTASTIC TEACHER RESOURCES

Each weekly Fiction Express episode comes with a PDF of teacher resources packed with ideas to extend the text.

"The teaching resources are fab and easily fill a whole week of literacy lessons!"
Rachel Humphries, teacher at Westacre Middle School

FICTI◌N EXPRESS

The Sand Witch
by Tommy Donbavand

When twins Chris and Ella are left to look after
their younger brother on a deserted beach, they
expect everything to be normal, boring in fact. But
then something extraordinary happens! Will the
Sand Witch succeed in passing on her sandy curse
in this exciting adventure?

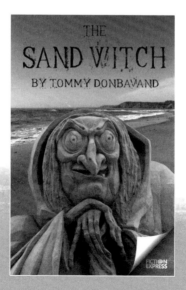

ISBN 978-1-783-22544-6

FICTI●N EXPRESS

Rise of the Rabbits
by Barry Hutchison

When twins Harvey and Lola are given the school rabbit, Mr Lugs, to look after for the weekend, they're both very excited. That is until the rabbit begins to mutate and decides the time has come for bunnies to rise up and seize control.

It's up to Harvey and Lola to find a way to return Mr Lugs and his friends to normal, before the mutant menaces sweep across the country – and then the world!

ISBN 978-1-78322-540-8

FICTI●N EXPRESS

Rémy Brunel and the Circus Horse
by Sharon Gosling

"Roll up, roll up, and see the greatest show on Earth!" Rémy Brunel loves her life in the circus – riding elephants, practising tightrope tricks and dazzling audiences. But when two new magicians arrive at the circus, everyone is wary of them. What exactly are they up to? What secrets are they trying to hide? Should Rémy and her new friend Matthias trust them?

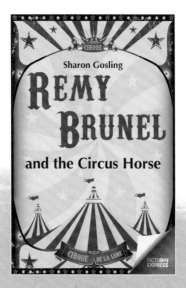

ISBN 978-1-783-22469-2

FICTION EXPRESS

The Time Detectives:
The Mystery of Maddie Musgrove
by Alex Woolf

When Joe Smallwood goes to stay with his Uncle Theo and cousin Maya life seems dull, until he finds a strange smartphone nestling beside a gravestone. The phone enables Joe and Maya to become time-travelling detectives and takes them on an exciting adventure back to Victorian times. Can they prove maidservant Maddie Musgrove's innocence? Can they save her from the gallows?

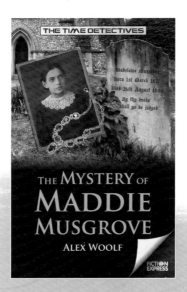

ISBN 978-1-783-22459-3

About the Author

Sunday Times bestseller Cavan Scott is the author of over 70 books and audio dramas, plus hundreds of comic strips. He has written *Doctor Who*, *The Sarah Jane Adventures*, *Adventure Time*, *Penguins of Madagascar*, *Moshi Monsters*, and *Power Rangers*. He also writes *Minnie the Minx*, *Roger the Dodger*, *Bananaman* and more for the world famous *Beano* comic.

Cavan lives in Bristol with his wife, two daughters and an inflatable Dalek called Desmond. He supports Bristol City Football Club and knows the secret identity of club mascot, Scrumpy, but is sworn to secrecy.